Lewis and the
MYSTERY
of the MISSING BONES

The DOGGY Detective Series - Book 1

Aidan Niles

Lewis and the Mystery of the Missing Bones
Copyright © 2022 Aidan Niles

Contents

1
Trouble at the Park

Hi, I'm Lewis and I used to be a rescue dog. But now I have a new family, a new home, and friends. I was living in a scary shelter until my boy, Nicholas, and his parents changed my life. Now I live on 85 Mountain Drive with a large yard, good food, and fresh water.

Today, I was off to the dog park for playtime. But when I arrived, no one was playing. I wagged my tail to say hi to Buster and the crew. My friend Ed stood by himself near a large clump of bushes. He was shaking, with his tail drooped and his ears lowered. Buster and the local pack glared at Ed.

"Why are you by yourself?" I asked.

"You should leave," Ed said. "Buster will

get mad at you for being my friend."

Ed was a dachshund, also called a hot dog. Everything about him was long: his body, his tail, his hair. Only his legs were short. Hunkered down, he had made himself as small as possible.

"What happened?" I asked.

"Buster thinks I stole his bone collection."

For a moment I felt torn. Buster and the local pack had welcomed me as a new friend when I first came to the dog park, but Ed was my best friend. We had been in the pound together and used to huddle against one another through the bars of our cages to keep warm. Like me, he was a rescue dog. Our new families were friends and had adopted us at the same event.

Buster's bone collection was legendary. His boy had carved designs on them along with Buster's name. They weren't just bones;

they were special bones. Everyone at the park knew about it, and those of us who had the opportunity to visit Buster's house and see the collection couldn't help but drool at the thought of it. I couldn't believe someone would have had the nerve to steal those bones.

"Did you?"

Ed looked at me with sad eyes. "Are you kidding? No!"

"Then why are you a suspect?"

"Because last week Buster asked me to help him move the collection. There was a raccoon hanging around the yard. Buster kept running out through the dog door to scare it away, but it kept coming back. It moved into the tree by the fence. Buster was worried it might steal the bones, so he decided to move them to a safer place. He said he trusted me because his mom and my mom are good friends. I'm the only one who knew the secret location, besides Buster. Buster said I stole the bones because I'm a rescue dog and rescue dogs often steal to get what they need."

"That's not true," I said, offended that Buster would say that. It wasn't our fault we lost our homes.

"I told him I hadn't touched his bones, but he wouldn't listen. I always thought we were good friends."

"Buster just wants to be mad at someone."

Ed shivered. "He's threatening to beat me up if I don't return them."

Ed barely came to Buster's knee. If Buster even sat on him, it could be curtains for poor Ed. I put my thinking cap on. There had to be something I could do to help. "Just because you helped move them doesn't mean that you had the *opportunity* to steal them," I said. I read mystery stories with Nicholas, and sometimes we watch mystery movies on TV. I'm pretty good at figuring out motive and whodunit.

"But I did, Lewis. I went back to Buster's house with my mom the next day. Buster was at the groomers, and as we were leaving, his mom gave my mom a bone as a present to take home. She said Buster had too many."

"Oh no!" I said.

"I didn't touch the bone. I knew it was part of Buster's collection," Ed said. "When Buster came over to my house, he saw the bone and snarled at me. I tried to explain. He told me his collection was stolen several days ago. Then he pointed his snout at me. 'You miserable liar! You did it!' he said."

"You would never steal from anyone," I said. I nuzzled Ed's neck to try to make him feel better.

Ed hung his head. "Thanks, Lewis, but if you stay here, Buster and the gang will punish you too."

"I'm going to talk with Buster and fix this," I told Ed. "Back in a flash!"

2
Buster's Bones

Buster and the gang glared at me as I trotted over to them. My paws started to sweat. I'm a small dog with curly white hair. People say I am a poodle mix or a poodix. Buster is huge and has a lot more friends. He is the leader of the local pack and runs the dog park.

"Why were you talking to the thief?" Buster growled. "You need to decide if you are one of us or not."

The rest of the pack grumbled in agreement. My legs trembled. I was pretty new to the pack and was scared of them being mad at me. I glanced back at Ed cowering by himself near the tree. As much as being alone scared me, I couldn't desert my best friend.

Taking a deep breath, I stared hard at Buster. "Ed is my friend," I said. "If he says he didn't steal your bones, then I believe him."

Buster sneered at me. "Maybe you're a thief too."

I took a step back. "I did not steal your bones."

"You're defending the thief."

"And you're not being fair," I said.

Buster put his face close to mine. His drool dripped onto my head. "Pick. Now!"

I gulped. "Ed didn't steal your bones, and I am going to prove it!"

The pack laughed at me.

"You're nothing but a silly rescue dog," a short-tailed corgi named Larry jeered. "Your people didn't care about you and got rid of you."

I winced. My first family had left me in

the dog pound. Sometimes really bad things happen in life. But I learned that those bad times pass, and I've always tried to make the best of things.

"What's wrong with being a rescue?" I asked. Nobody answered. "I'm done watching you bully my friend."

Turning away from Buster and the pack, I walked back to Ed. "Hey," I said. "We have work to do."

Ed lifted his head and stood tall on his stubby legs. "You don't have to help, Lewis. It's fine."

"You're my best friend."

Ed smiled, his tongue hanging out of his mouth. "Do you have a plan?"

"Detectives always start by asking questions."

"But everybody thinks I did it. You're the only one who believes me," Ed said, ears drooping.

"That doesn't mean anything," I said. "All detectives know that you need proof, and they don't have any. Just because the pack believes a rumor doesn't make it true."

"My friends used to say that cats were mean and scary, but since Whiskers moved into the house, I discovered that cats are pretty cool. She knocks tasty treats off the counter for me during meals, even if she is kind of bossy," Ed said.

"Ask Whiskers to stop by my house this evening."

"How will that help us?"

I scratched the itch under my collar. "We're stuck in our yards. Whiskers has unsupervised walking privileges."

"Got it," Ed said, nodding his head. "What exactly is your plan?"

"Buster moved his bones because of the raccoon in his yard. The raccoon is a possible suspect that we need to question," I said.

"We can't talk to a raccoon, Lewis! Raccoons are trouble."

"He's right, you know. Raccoons are bad news," came a singsong voice from the tree.

Ed turned in circles barking an alert to the pack. Nobody came.

"Looks like you're on your own," the voice said.

3
Squirrel!

"Missing bones? You don't say. I prefer nuts."
Staring down from a long lower branch of the
tree was a gray squirrel with a bushy tail.

"Do you know where the bones are?" I
asked.

The squirrel turned in a circle, paused,
and then whirled twice more. "Nope. But last
week I found this."

He scampered off and quickly returned
with a small rubber ball.

"It tastes terrible, like acorns gone off. Of
course, it is fun to play with." He dropped the
ball on Ed's head.

"Hey!" Ed yelped.

"FETCH the ball. Good doggie."

When Ed didn't move, the squirrel

scratched his head. "Why aren't you fetching? That's what dogs do, isn't it?"

"How am I supposed to return it to you? Dogs can't climb!" Ed grumbled.

The squirrel paused. "I hadn't considered that."

"I'd wait to retrieve your ball until all the dogs leave. Dogs love chasing squirrels," I said.

"That's why I stay high in my tree. But it's so lonely up here," the squirrel said. "Are you sure you can't climb? Have you tried it?"

"Don't other squirrels live in this park?" Ed asked.

"No. Too many dogs. That's why this wonderful tree wasn't already spoken for. Great view, plentiful food, a private pool … what's not to love? But I hide when the dogs arrive."

"You're the first squirrel I've talked to,"

I said. "I'm Lewis and this is my friend Ed."

"Dogs don't normally have anything nice to say. It makes finding friends hard."

"You might have better luck if you stop dropping balls on their heads," Ed muttered.

"What's your name?" I asked.

"Everyone calls me Phil. So how do you plan to find these missing bones?"

"By investigating."

Phil scurried down to a lower branch. "That sounds interesting. Can I help?"

"We need all the help we can get."

Phil chittered happily. "What do you need?"

"Keep your furry ears open for dog gossip about Buster's missing bones."

"I can do that. Although it doesn't sound as fun as boinking them on their heads."

Ed rolled his eyes and sighed. He looked ready to say something, but I stopped him with a glare.

"Detectives can't solve the case without information," I said.

Phil nodded. "I'm a great listener when I'm not talking."

"We're counting on you, Phil!" I said. I gave Ed a nudge.

"Yeah. Thanks for your help," Ed said.

"Happy to help. I was going to say something, but now I can't remember. Maybe I will remember in a minute." Phil's eyes widened. "You have company. Gotta run!" With a quick flick of his tail, he disappeared into the higher branches of the tree.

4

The Investigation Begins

Nicholas was walking toward me with the leash. "Leave the poor squirrel alone; we've got to go home. What do you say after dinner we watch the rest of that mystery?"

I wagged my tail while Nicholas hooked my collar. "Don't forget to ask Whiskers to stop by my yard tonight," I called out to Ed as Nicholas led me out of the park.

Back home, I kept Nicholas company while he did his math homework. A rather loud meowing broke the silence. I hopped off our bed and ran to my yard. There on the fence post sat Whiskers, her long black tail swishing. "It took you long enough."

"Hi, Whiskers. Good to see you too."

Whiskers leapt lightly to the ground next to me. "My pleasure. Thanks for standing up for my Ed. Buster is foolish, but I can't fix him." Whiskers rolled her eyes and sighed. "So how do we help?"

"We find out what really happened to the bones."

"That'll use up at least two of my nine lives."

"Who do you know? Detectives interview anyone with legs. You never know who has seen or heard something."

"Makes sense. I can ask some of the cats that live near Buster and see if they've seen or heard anything. Buster had a lot of bones according to Ed. Moving them would take some time."

"Tell them to spread the word. That many bones don't just disappear into thin air without a trace. Can you spring me from this yard so I can ask a few questions of my own?"

"Your family better not find out! They won't like it."

I swallowed hard. I didn't want to upset my new family, but Ed needed my help. "I'll be careful."

Whiskers jumped onto the gate, and with a flick of her paw, the small metal latch clicked. The gate swung open. I pushed a rock between the door and the post so I wouldn't be locked out of my yard. With any luck, I would be back in time for movies and popcorn.

"Ready?" Whiskered asked.

"Let's roll," I said, following her out of the gate.

We crept down the street and cut over to behind the water towers. "This is where we part ways," Whiskers said once we arrived on Buster's block. "Fair warning: Dogs and raccoons don't get along. You might think about that before you go barking up that tree."

"Thanks for everything, Whiskers."

She nodded. "Good luck and be careful of cars and skateboards when you're walking home. Things with wheels are an animal's worst nightmare."

Steeling my nerves, I walked towards Buster's house, stopping just out of sight of the windows. If Buster discovered me, I wouldn't get the chance to question this possible witness.

I found the tree where the raccoon

resided. Empty bags and crushed cans lay scattered across the ground. My nose wrinkled at the smell, a mixture of old food and damp earth.

"Hello? Anyone home?"

Silence.

"Hellooo? Woof? Calling all raccoons!" No answer. Sniffing around the tree, my nose caught a faint scent. I followed it into the blackberry bushes. Crawling on my belly, I inched my way through the prickly branches. I spied a small pile of white bones. My heart leapt. I found them! I crawled faster. These bones would prove Ed's innocence.

"Grrrr … Grrr …"

"Woof … woof?" I asked, hoping for a friendly response.

"Get out of my territory!" A tough-looking raccoon was baring its big teeth. Seeing its black mask, sharp-looking claws, and hackles raised, my legs started to shake.

"Is that your tree over there? I'm looking for Buster's missing bones."

"I said get out!" The raccoon lunged.

Paws scrabbling, I scooted as fast as a greyhound out from under the bush and ran for the road.

"On your left! Car!" a voice called out.

5
Caught

I skidded to a stop at the curb in the nick of time, my heart pounding and my tail tucked between my legs.

"I told you to be careful of wheels!" Whiskers slinked out from under a bush.

"Thanks for the warning! I was running away from a vicious raccoon. Detectives aren't allowed to panic. I guess I'm a wimp."

"You're doing great. This is your first case. You'll get better with practice."

"How can you be sure?" I asked.

"Because I am a cat. I'm sure about everything, even when I'm wrong. But I'm never wrong. Ask Ed."

"What about the time you–"

"That never happened, and I'm not discussing it again," Whiskers said. "Focus on the case. I would tell Buster that the raccoon did it. Raccoons are bad news. Everyone knows it."

"Remember, innocent until proven guilty. We don't want to be like Buster. We need evidence."

Whiskers sighed. "I had a feeling you were going to say that. You and your sense of honor. It's so much easier to blame bad things on those we don't like."

"Did you hear anything from the cat community?"

"Nothing."

"Let's try to find another lead. Otherwise, I am going to have to try to talk to that raccoon again." Just thinking about it made me shudder.

"Gotcha!" A strong pair of hands grabbed me and lifted me up. "You're the little dog that the Smiths adopted. You shouldn't be out."

Whiskers yowled and hissed at the man.

Struggling, I tried to tell him that I was a detective and that I had places to go, but he couldn't understand me.

"Don't be scared," he said, gently patting my head.

Realizing he was determined to rescue me, I gave him a small lick of thanks.

"Why are you thanking him?" Whiskers asked. "He's ruining everything!"

"He doesn't speak dog or cat and he thinks he's helping," I said. "And if you haven't noticed, he's bigger than both of us. I'm going to be rescued whether I need it or not."

He patted my head again. "I'm not going to hurt your friend," he told Whiskers. "I'm just going to bring him home where he'll be safe."

"Not helpful, human," Whiskers said.

The man just smiled. "Go on home, kitty."

Tail twitching with annoyance, Whiskers turned to leave. "I'll stop by later, Lewis. As soon as you get home, push the rock away and let the gate close. I'll open it again.

Humans. So annoying." She gave the man a dirty look.

The man stuffed me into the car and drove me back to my house. I was going to be in so much trouble.

The man carried me to the front door and rang the bell.

Nicholas opened it and stared at us in surprise. "Hi, Mr. Lopez. Lewis? How did you get out?"

"Hi, Nick," the man called Mr. Lopez said. "I found him a few blocks over. I almost hit him with my car." He handed me to Nicholas.

"Thank you for bringing him home. I don't know how he got out."

"I would check the yard. Make sure no one left the gate open."

"I will. Thank you so much for bringing him back."

Nicholas put me down, and I ran for the yard, barking loudly as I pretended that I heard something. I needed to close the gate before Nicholas checked the yard. Using my snout, I pushed the rock away and the gate swung shut. I barked several more times until Nicholas came into the yard. Head down, I whimpered as I belly crawled toward him to show him I was sorry.

"How did you get out, Lewis?" he asked, scratching my ears.

I gave him my best innocent look and followed him as he began checking the fence line. I held my breath as he reached for the gate and gave it a shake. "Everything looks okay," he said, giving me a puzzled look. "So how did you get out?"

I wagged my tail at him.

"You must have snuck out the front door when mom left to run errands."

I followed him back into the house and stayed with him while he finished his homework. I felt guilty for causing Nicholas worry. I wanted to be a good dog, but I had to help Ed.

After dinner, Nicholas put on a detective movie, and we snuggled on the couch. "I'm going to be a detective when I grow up," he said, stroking my fur. "You can help me."

I liked the idea a lot. I wished I could ask Nicholas for help with the missing bones, but he needed to learn how to speak *dog*.

The detective in the movie asked a lot of questions and collected clues until he was finally able to solve the mystery. That's what I needed to do tomorrow. Ask more questions and collect clues. I still wasn't sure what I was looking for, but I was hoping I'd know when I saw or heard it. When the movie ended, Nicholas and I went to bed.

I listened for Whiskers, but when I didn't hear her, I finally drifted off to sleep. I was trapped until Whiskers could let me out again.

6
Friends in High Places

Saturday is my favorite day of the week because Nicholas walks me *before* he plays with his friends. He always takes me to the park, and today was no exception.

Nicholas unhooked me from the leash. Ed was hanging out near the tree. I figured he must be talking to Phil. Buster, Monte, and the rest of the gang were chasing each other and a bunch of balls, one of which rolled to my paws.

"Hi, Monte," I said to the terrier chasing the ball.

Monte shot me an apologetic smile. "Sorry, Lewis, but Buster says we can't play with you anymore."

I shrank away and walked over to Ed, my ears drooping.

"Monte gave you the cold shoulder too," Ed said. "This is my fault."

"*You* didn't steal the bones! Buster is mean."

"Yeah, well in the meantime it looks like it is you, me, and … Phil."

Phil slipped an acorn in the acorn hole in the tree trunk. "Hi, Lewis."

"Hey, Phil," I said. "I have news on our investigation."

"I love news!" Phil said, his eyes wide.

I told Ed and Phil about my trip to the tree near Buster's house, the angry raccoon, and the pile of bones. "I'm scared to go back, but unless I can find another clue, I'm going to have to be brave and take a closer look."

"It's so frustrating that I can't leave the yard. I should go with you," Ed said.

"I'd help too, but I tend to get lost," Phil

said. "I'm not good with directions."

"Whiskers and I have this covered."

"She has unsupervised walking privileges," Ed sighed. "I don't know why humans think cats are more responsible than dogs."

"It's because cats play fetch," Phil said, holding his rubber ball.

"Cats don't fetch," Ed said. "And I am not doing that no matter what you say."

Confused, I looked back and forth between Ed and Phil.

"He wants to drop the ball on my head," Ed said grumpily.

"Because it's funny," Phil said. "I offered to play fetch, but you said no."

"Ed can't climb, remember?" I said.

"I explained that to him," Ed whispered to me. "Sort of."

Phil appeared to think for a moment. "Can I drop the ball on your head, Lewis?"

"No, but I promise to play fetch with you."

"Can you climb?"

"No, but we'll play one day when it's safe for you to come down the tree."

"Really?" Phil asked excitedly as he ran back and forth on the branch.

"Really, Phil. I like fetch."

"Oh thank you, Lewis! I'll find a way. Of course, those mean dogs will have to leave before we can play, but … Oh, that reminds me. I spoke with Pepin the Short yesterday. He lives right up in the open space. He won't visit me here in the dog park, so I visited him. His hill is so big, I didn't have to worry about missing it. I asked him about the bones. Did you know that Pepin forgot where he buried most of his nuts? I helped him look for them. There sure are a lot of trees in his forest."

Phil rambled on and on and on about the problem of lost nuts.

"Interrupt him, Lewis. He's eating up our time."

"Uh, Phil?"

"Yes?"

"Did Pepin the Short have a clue about Buster's missing bones?"

"Pepin knows a lot about a lot of things," Phil said.

"What did he say?" I asked.

"He told me he saw a bunch of bones in the open space near the water towers," Phil said, pointing out a familiar hill.

"That's Buster's hill," Ed said.

I nodded. "Did he say anything else?"

Phil thought about it for a moment. "He said that the field attracts too many people, and he doesn't like all the noise."

"Thanks, Phil."

"You're welcome. Was I helpful?"

"I think you were."

Phil smiled. "Oh goody. I love being

helpful. Are you sure I can't drop the ball on Ed's head?"

"I know I'm going to regret this, but go ahead," Ed said.

Ed squinched his eyes shut and waited for the ball to drop. But Phil just stared at Ed, waiting until he opened his eyes.

"Drop it already!" Ed said.

"No. I have no way to get it back until everyone leaves. I keep forgetting about that part. But it means so much to me that you were willing to let me."

"Another time then," Ed said. "Tell Pepin we appreciate his clue about the bones and that he can count on Lewis and me if he ever needs our help."

"Oh, thank you, Ed. You are a good dog! I like you a lot."

Ed looked embarrassed. "Thanks, Phil. I like you too. I think."

Phil looked pleased. "So, what do we do now?"

"We follow Pepin the Short's lead and go to the field. It's a safer clue than visiting the raccoon again," I said.

"Be careful, Lewis. Whiskers told me about you getting caught."

"I will be. I don't want to make my family worry, but we can't let Buster bully you."

Nicholas called my name. "I've got to go. See you guys on the next park day?"

"Oh yes!" Phil said.

As Ed and I ran to where Nicholas was waiting, I said, "tell Whiskers to open my gate again. Nicholas has a soccer game, so I'll have free time."

7
The Plan

When Nicholas and the rest of the family left for the soccer game, I went to the backyard. The gate was still locked. Why hadn't Whiskers opened it? I called her name.

"Don't be in such a hurry," an orange tabby cat said, hopping onto the fence. "Whiskers said not to open the gate until after your people left. I watched them check the yard earlier." With a flick of his paw, he opened the latch. I pushed the rock back into place to make sure it remained opened.

"Thanks for your help," I said.

"Whiskers said you were cool. I'm Red. I live two houses over. If you get stuck just holler and I'll come and let you out. Never met a dog detective before."

"I'm not sure I am one, but I want to be someday. Right now, I just need to help my friend Ed."

"Good luck to you. Holler if you get stuck," Red said.

This time I made sure to hide from people and watch for cars as I walked to Ed and Whiskers' house. "Ed? Whiskers? Are you home?"

"Over here, Lewis!" Ed said.

Ed's nose poked through the white picket fence. We greeted each other with a friendly sniff. Staring at him through the wooden slats reminded me of our days in the pound. "Nicholas is at soccer so I was hoping

Whiskers could come with me to check out Phil's lead."

"Whiskers is in the house taking a nap," Ed said. "I wish I could go with you. It's my fault that Buster is mad at you."

"Buster is a bully, Ed. You didn't do anything wrong."

"I know, but this isn't your fight."

"Friends look out for one another," I reminded him. "We are going to find Buster's bones and clear your name. I promise."

"Thanks, Lewis. I'll get Whiskers."

"No need. You two are loud," Whiskers said. With a single leap, she perched on top of the fence railing. She licked her paw and used it to groom her face. "What's the plan?"

"I'm headed to the open space to look for the bones Phil said his friend saw there."

"I told Whiskers everything that happened at the park," Ed said.

Whiskers rolled her eyes. "Do *not* let that squirrel drop things on your head."

"I was trying to be nice," Ed grumbled.

"Don't confuse niceness with foolishness. You could get hurt," Whiskers said.

Ed grinned. "She loves me."

"Dogs!" Whiskers snorted. "I take it you want my help, Lewis?"

"Can you come?"

"Do you know where you're going?" Whiskers asked.

"The field near the water towers."

Whiskers leapt to the ground. "Keep the family amused while I go with Lewis," she said to Ed.

"I wish I could come," Ed said.

"I still haven't figured out how to open your gate," Whiskers reminded him.

Ed pressed his nose through the fence. "You both be careful."

"We will. See you later," I said.

Whiskers took the lead. "Let's cut through the space behind Buster's house."

I was afraid of running into Buster, but I followed Whiskers. We had to check out the lead. I cringed when I saw Buster sunning himself in the yard.

Whiskers hissed as Buster charged the fence.

"Get away from my house!" Buster yelled.

"Just passing by," I said. "Going to check out a lead on your missing bones."

Buster growled. "You aren't supposed to be out of your yard. Maybe Ed had you steal my bones."

"I didn't steal your bones. I am a

detective, Buster. To find your bones I have to investigate."

"You are a nobody, and now you are hanging out with a cat."

"Whiskers is my friend, and she is helping me to find your bones!"

"That's not true, Lewis," Whiskers said. "I am helping to prove Ed innocent. I wouldn't help you, Buster." Whiskers stuck her nose in the air.

"I don't care. I want you gone," Buster growled. "I spent years collecting those bones!"

Annoyed, I stared at Buster through the fence. "That isn't my fault! You're a jerk. Why don't you try helping for a change?" I said.

"I'm the pack leader. You can't talk to me that way!"

"He just did," Whiskers said. "Let's go,

Lewis. We've got work."

"Maybe if you helped us, we could find your bones sooner." I looked at Buster hoping he might offer up a clue.

"I know who took my bones," Buster growled. "Ed helped me carry them into the house. He stole them when I was gone. Now he has to pay, and I'm going to make you pay too!"

Buster turned and disappeared through the dog door.

I took off after Whiskers thinking about what Buster said. "Who could have gotten into Buster's house and taken the bones?"

"Anyone willing to crawl through the dog door," Whiskers said.

"That means there might be clues in Buster's house."

Whiskers nodded. "Buster won't help us if that's what you're thinking. We have to do this on our own."

"Which means we need to get to that field."

We passed under some tall trees, careful to avoid a group of people walking nearby. I could see the water towers just ahead. "I hope Pepin the Short is right."

"Me too," Whiskers said.

8
Disaster Strikes

We tiptoed out from the trees and into the open space. A loud buzzing like a gang of mosquitoes bit at our ears. "Look out!" I yelled, pointing at a winged monster darting above our heads.

Whisker yelped and jumped up on her hind legs. She batted at the scary thing. It zoomed out past her tail and circled back. Whiskers took another swipe and missed.

Several boys were standing nearby. One of them laughed. "Watch this!"

The object tried to bite Whiskers again. She spun and tried to bat it with her paw.

"Whiskers, let's hide in the trees," I said.

"No! I can get it. I know I can."

I knew she wouldn't leave until she had caught it. I waited for the object to buzz down again and that's when I sprung up and caught it in my mouth.

"Hey, give me back my drone," a boy with brown hair screamed and bolted toward us.

Oops! We were in trouble! I dropped the toy and ran for the trees, my heart pounding. Phew. The boy couldn't catch us. We hid behind a tree trunk.

"You must be Phil's friends," came a voice from above.

"Pepin the Short?" I asked.

A tiny squirrel with a long fluffy tail peeked at us from a tree nest. "That's me. Who's the cat? Phil said his friends were dogs."

"This is Whiskers. She lives with Ed, and she's helping me find the missing bones."

Pepin laughed. "You're not going to find them here. This is where the drones fly. The place is really noisy but still better than living in Phil's dog park. I don't understand why he won't move."

My heart sank. "You didn't see any bones around here?"

"Is it safe for me to come down?"

Whiskers nodded. "Don't worry. I'm done playing chase for the day."

Pepin scurried down the trunk and sat on the ground next to us. "Phil gets a bit confused sometimes. I told him I didn't know anything about missing bones, but if he wanted drones, I could point him to a field full of them," he said. "What do you want with a bunch of old bones?"

I explained the bone mystery. Pepin listened and gathered a pile of nuts. "If you want information, you should talk to the raccoons. They know the dirt on everything.

They're always going through human trash cans. There's one that lives in the bushes near Buster's house."

Whiskers and I thanked Pepin.

"It looks like we're going to have to go back to that raccoon," Whiskers said.

I shuddered. The thought of being on the pointy end of those sharp teeth made me question my courage as a detective. Ed's face swam into my mind. I couldn't fail my best friend.

As we snuck past Buster's house, he jumped at the fence, eyes blazing. "Tell Ed I'll see you guys at the park tomorrow."

I looked at Whiskers. On second thought, Buster scared me more.

9

The Furry and the Furious

"Why are you moving so slow, Lewis?" Nicholas asked. "Come on. We're going to the park. Your favorite place. Ed will be there."

When I sat back on my rump, Nicholas gently tugged the leash. Reluctantly I walked faster.

Buster was there, of course. King of the Park. I was scared. "Go play, Lewis," Nicholas said, letting me off the leash.

I was not budging. Buster and the gang

were running in circles, and Buster glared at me every time he circled by us.

Ed arrived a couple of minutes later and plopped next to me. "He's going to get us eventually."

"I know," I said glumly. "I used to love coming to the park, and now it's awful. I hate being afraid."

"Me too," said Ed.

The more I watched everyone play and chase the ball, the angrier I got. It wasn't fair! Buster didn't own the park. "You know what? I'm going to go visit Phil," I said.

Tail held high, I ran over to the tree and Ed followed.

"Took you guys long enough," Phil said. "What were you doing? I've been waiting for you."

"Sorry, Phil. Buster is pretty mad at us right now," I said.

"That's not good. Not good at all. I've seen dog fights, and you little guys always lose."

"That's not helping, Phil," Ed said.

"You need help? I will help. I'll be right back. Try not to die. Buster is coming over."

Ed's tail drooped. I gave him a nudge. "Look tough."

"Where? At his knees?" Ed said. He stood as tall as a dachshund mix could stand.

"What's up, Buster?" I asked.

There was slobber at the corners of Buster's mouth. "Leave my park!" he growled.

I moved away to avoid the drool that threatened to land on my head. "This isn't *your* park," I told him.

He snarled, but I held my ground. His muscles bunched in his haunches.

"You'll get into trouble," Ed said.

Buster lunged and bared his teeth. "Maybe it will be worth it," he said.

"Never fear! Phil is here!"

Buster looked up just before the red rubber ball hit him between the eyes. He yelped and hurled himself at the tree trunk. Buster was big and strong, but he couldn't climb, and he didn't possess the slightest jumping ability.

Phil danced on the branch above Buster. He took aim with a flurry of nuts. "That's right, dog. Jump!" Phil grinned at Ed and me. "This is so much fun."

"Uh, Buster?" I said. "Everyone is laughing at you."

Buster whipped around. "Whatever," he said. "Stay in your tree, squirrel, because if I catch you …"

Phil dropped a nut on his head. "Leave my friends alone. I don't like you! If you hurt Lewis and Ed, I'm going to tell all the squirrels to drop things on your head when you're at home."

Buster slunk off like an angry monster.

"Phil, you were amazing," I said. "You saved us from Buster."

"I was amazing, wasn't I? You'll tell everyone about it, right? That would be nice for me. If I tell them, no one will believe me, but if you guys tell the story of Phil the Brave, they'll be impressed."

"I'll tell Whiskers tonight," Ed said. "Thanks. You're the best. We owe you."

Phil nodded. "I liked saving you. It felt good. Did you find the bones?"

"No. Pepin saw *drones* in the field, not bones," I said.

Phil looked sad. "Darn. I really wanted it to be bones."

"It's okay, Phil. It was a good lead."

"So, what do you do now?" Phil asked.

"I have to visit the scary raccoon."

"I don't know if that's such a good idea, Lewis," Ed said.

"Maybe not, but Phil won't be able to protect us from Buster forever. We have to find those bones or things will never get better."

Ed's ears drooped. "Why does everything have to be so hard and unfair?"

"I don't know, but I heard my new mom tell Nicholas that life is hard sometimes and we just have to suck it up and move forward."

"I don't know what that means," Phil said.

Ed sniffled. "It means Lewis has to have a chat with the raccoons."

10
Prime Suspects

"I didn't do it. I swear I didn't do it. Mrs. McCutcheon treated me right," the man on the television said.

I listened to the suspect proclaim his innocence as the detective asked the man question after question while looking around the room searching for clues.

"Who do you think did it?" Nicholas asked me. "I think it was Mrs. Brady."

I wanted to say Mr. Tompkins because he scared me, but there wasn't enough evidence to support that theory, and Mrs. Brady had a motive. Mrs. McCutcheon had stolen her pie recipe. In the end, Mrs. Brady was the culprit. Mrs. McCutcheon had sold Mrs. Brady's pie recipe to a big company for a lot of money, and Mrs. Brady, unable to prove the theft, had wanted revenge so she'd invented the bad luck ghost to haunt her.

Nicholas turned off the television and crawled into bed. I waited until he fell asleep. I needed to meet Whiskers. It was time to talk to the raccoon with the bones.

Whiskers was waiting for me on her fence. Ed slumped on the ground. "I don't know about this, Lewis," Ed said. "Raccoons are dangerous."

"So is Buster," I said. "This is the only lead we have. We have to follow it." I was scared, but a detective did what was needed to solve the case.

"Get me out of here, Whiskers!" Ed demanded.

"I'm a cat, not a miracle worker. Our fence has a bolt, not a latch. Sorry, Ed. But you know where to take our people if something goes wrong."

Ed began pacing. "This is a bad idea. It's dark out there."

"I can see in the dark, Ed. I'm a cat. I'll look after Lewis."

"I'm worried about you too!" Ed said.

Whiskers purred. "I know. I love you too, Ed. Don't stress about it."

Whiskers jumped off the fence and landed without a sound next to me. "Let's roll," she said.

Everything looked different at night. The trees stretched their shadowy branches, allowing a small glimmer of moonlight to pass. The air was heavy with silence, disturbed only by the tune of crickets.

Whiskers and I walked to the brushy area where I had seen the raccoon with the bones. "I think this is it," I said. I could barely make out the clump of prickly bushes.

"I'll keep a lookout for trouble," Whiskers said.

I belly crawled under the brush, sniffing as I went. The smell I remembered was still there, but faint. The bushes blocked even the light from the moon and stars. Fortunately, I have an excellent nose, and I put it to good use as I hunted for Buster's bones. Excitement poured through me as the smell got stronger. The bones must still be here!

"Get out of my home," a voice hissed.

"I'm looking for missing bones."

The voice snorted. "I don't know anything about missing bones, but if you want those bones, take them. There isn't any meat left."

I reached a pocket in the brush. A small yet fierce-looking raccoon stood over a nursery of kits. Nearby lay a pile of bones, perfectly cleaned and neatly stacked.

"My name is Tilda. You must be awfully hungry to try to take bare chicken bones from my kits."

"I'm Lewis. I'm a detective."

I inspected the bones. Tilda told the truth. These weren't Buster's bones. I should have known better. My heart sank. My last lead was gone.

"The garbage can in front of the yellow house has some decent scraps. Nothing like chicken meat, but it will get you by," Tilda said.

"Thanks, Tilda, but I wasn't looking for food. Buster's bone collection has been stolen, and I'm trying to find it. "

"Someone stole Blustery Buster's old bones?" Tilda laughed. "Why would anyone want old bones with no meat on them?"

"It's a dog thing. Buster thinks my friend Ed stole those bones, and he's making Ed's life miserable."

"Buster isn't keen on us raccoons either. Sorry I can't help you."

"Sorry for invading your home. I was so

busy looking for the bones, I forgot that I was trespassing."

I had been so scared of Tilda because she was a raccoon, only to discover that she was rather friendly when given the chance.

"I wish you luck. I've got to hurry. I'm teaching these kits of mine how to scavenge. Are you sure you don't want these bones?"

"I'm sure," I said. "Thanks again."

I crawled out from the brush.

"What took you so long?" Whiskers asked. "I was starting to get nervous. You didn't find the bones, did you?"

"No. They were just chicken bones."

"Well, I'm glad that you didn't run into any trouble," Whiskers said as we walked back to her house.

"No trouble. Just a nice raccoon named Tilda and her kits."

"You ran into a raccoon? And she was nice? Then why do my people always complain about them? I think they look scary with those black masks and sharp teeth. Did she help you?"

I shook my head. "She was surprised that anyone would want Buster's dirty bones."

"Why?"

"Raccoons want food, not an old bone collection."

"That makes sense. So, what do we do now?"

"We go home."

When we reached Whisker's house, she jumped up on the fence.

"You didn't find anything, did you?" Ed said with a sigh.

Whiskers hung her head. "I'm sorry, Ed. I know how much you want to clear your name."

"I do," Ed said. "But I was more worried about you and Lewis. Mom gave me a big steak bone tonight. I saved it for you, Lewis."

"Thanks, Ed. I hope you don't mind if I give it to someone who could really use it."

Ed pushed the meaty bone through the fence.

"You're going back there now?" Whiskers asked.

"I want to give her the bone while the meat is still fresh. Everyone needs somebody looking out for them."

Whiskers sighed. "I'll be back, Ed."

Together, Whiskers and I brought the bone to Tilda's. She must have been out scavenging with her kits, so we left the meat next to the chicken bones.

I was out of leads. Back home, I crawled back into bed with Nicholas. There had to be something I was missing. The bones had been in Buster's house. Yawning, I decided to search the area for clues tomorrow, before drifting off to sleep.

11
The Missing Link

"See you later, Lewis," Nicholas said as he ran out the door. Monday mornings were always busy as Mom and Dad rushed to get ready for work and drop Nicholas off at school.

I waited until I heard the cars leave the driveway before I sneaked out of the yard and walked to Buster's house. The streets were lined with garbage cans, blue recycling bins, and green compost cans. The garbage trucks would be out collecting around the neighborhood in a few hours.

The first yard I stopped by belonged to a reddish terrier mix named June. I explained my mission and asked if she had seen Buster's bones.

"No, but you might want to check with Reggie on the corner. He sits in the yard all day long. If something happens on this block, he'll know about it," she said.

"Thanks, June."

Reggie was laying on the porch when I walked up to his fence.

"I'm looking for some missing bones."

"You and everyone else," Reggie said, ambling across the yard.

"Who else is looking?" I asked.

"A couple of raccoons were talking about

a bunch of bones. Of course, raccoons are always talking about food. Them, and the birds. Hard to take a nap with all the chattering."

"But you haven't heard anything about Buster's missing bones?"

"Besides the fact that they are missing? Sorry. I wish you luck finding them," Reggie said.

"If you hear anything, don't hesitate to bark."

"Sure thing, Lewis. Come by and see me again. I don't walk too much anymore, but I do like the company."

How could a collection of bones disappear into thin air? I wondered as I walked back toward Buster's house.

A cleaning lady with a bag of trash came out of the house next to June's. She removed the lid and stuffed the garbage into the can.

Could it be? It had to be. It was the only answer that made sense! I ran to Ed's house and called for him and Whiskers. They met me in the yard, and I told them my theory.

"We're going to need help," Whiskers said.

Together we sprinted to Buster's house. He was in his backyard sunbathing.

"Buster!" I called. "I think I know where your bones are."

"Of course you do. You helped Ed take them," he grumbled.

"Meet me in your front yard in ten minutes."

"You better not be wasting my time, Lewis," Buster said.

"I'm not!" I said.

At the front of the house, Whiskers and I

tried to open the compost can, but it had been strapped shut with bungee cords.

"We're going to have to tip it," I said.

"There are going to be some really mad people if we get caught, Lewis," Whiskers said.

"We don't have a choice. The trucks will be coming soon."

I hurled myself at the can, but I was unable to knock it over.

Buster walked into the front yard as I failed once again. "What the heck are you doing?" he asked, growling at me. "Leave my trash alone!"

"I think your bones are in the compost."

"Why would anyone throw away my bones?"

"To you they're valuable, but to others, they're just a bunch of bones. Someone else besides Ed knew where the bones were."

"How do you know?" Buster asked.

"Ed said that your mother gave him a bone to take home. She said that you had too many. That means she must have found your bones. I'm guessing she threw them away. Humans are always cleaning."

"You would say anything to help Ed. Besides, you have no proof," Buster said.

"The proof is in the cans," Whiskers said. "Think about it, Buster. It makes sense."

"Maybe, but so does the fact that Ed stole my bones. I found good hiding places. Only Ed knew where they all were."

Buster was refusing to listen, and without help, I couldn't open the garbage cans to see if I was right.

"You wasted my time, Lewis."

"Don't leave just yet," a familiar voice

said. Tilda and her kits were walking towards us. She held her hands up and wiggled her fingers. "I'm pretty good with cords."

Whiskers jumped down from the can, and Tilda climbed up. "If I find your bones, Buster, you will apologize to Lewis and Ed in front of the whole neighborhood. And share your treats with me occasionally," Tilda said.

"If those bones aren't in there, you will move away from my house. I don't like raccoons."

Tilda unhooked the cords. She and her kits lifted the lid. Scraps of roast chicken, rotting leaves, and vegetable peels flew through the air and landed all over the ground.

Tilda stopped digging. She grunted as she yanked something out of the compost and held it behind her back. "Say please, Buster," she said.

"To a raccoon? I don't think so!"

"You're going to want the prize I found. Believe me."

"Fine!" Buster growled. "Just this once. Please."

Tilda tossed the object into Buster's yard.

"My bone!" Buster said, pouncing on it.

"Looks like you'll be apologizing at the park this afternoon," I said.

"Get me the rest of my bones first," Buster said.

"We said we'd prove that Ed didn't steal your bones, not that we would paw-deliver them to you," I said.

"You better not let the trucks take my bones away!"

"You were awful, Buster. If you want your bones back, share your treats with Tilda and her kits. If she hadn't agreed to help, your bones would still be lost."

Tilda raised her brows. Whiskers laughed.

Buster sat back on his haunches, looking stubborn until he heard the rumble of the garbage trucks. His eyes flicked between Tilda, Whiskers, and me. Finally, he spoke.

"Deal. I'll give you one steak bone a month for the next six months."

"Push it through the fence on Sunday nights," Tilda said.

Tilda pulled the bones out of the can. I handed the bones to Buster, while Whiskers supervised and kept an eye out for humans. Buster secreted each bone away. We didn't see his new hiding place.

When we were done with our mission, we walked Tilda and her kits home.

"Thanks again for your help today," I said. "You were impressive dealing with those bungee cords."

"Thank you for the bone you left me. That was really nice."

"You're welcome. See you around?"

"I hope so," Tilda said, disappearing into the brush with her kits.

"Looks like you have a knack for detective work after all. You solved the mystery of the missing bones," Whiskers said. "So, Detective Lewis, how did you figure out they were in the trash?"

"It all came together when I saw the lady taking her trash out. One of the first things Ed told me was that Buster's mother gave him a bone to take home with him. That meant that she knew the hiding place, which meant the bones were hidden in the house. And then Tilda asked why anyone would want dirty old bones with no meat on them. That meant that the bones didn't have any value to the animals most likely to steal them. And we know none of the neighborhood dogs would touch them. That left the humans as the only possible suspects. Humans throw out anything they consider to be old and dirty. That's how I deduced that the bones were in the compost."

"For a dog, you're pretty smart," Whiskers said.

"I couldn't have done it without you," I said.

"I know." Whiskers smiled. "Now let's go home and tell Ed the good news."

The End

About the Author

Children's book author Aidan Niles has always loved to write stories. He was inspired to write his new release Lewis and the Mystery of the Bones by his own dog, Lewis. His dog doesn't actually solve mysteries, like the book's main character, but Aidan and his family taught Lewis to talk using speech buttons and now the pup bullies everyone for walks, treats, and extra belly rubs.

One of the most surprising things Aidan learned in penning his debut book is how much time he spent editing and how little help his dog gave him. Writing is in Aidan's genes; his mother is a romance novelist and fostered his early love of storytelling. He hopes his young readers will come away from his books having escaped from the world to be entertained for a while and having learned something from his characters' journey that stays with them long after the book is closed.

Currently a student at the University of Chicago, Aidan loves languages and speaks Spanish and Russian and is learning Arabic. He is the editor-in-chief of The Majalla, an Arabic magazine. Other interests include anime, gaming, and most other nerdy endeavors. During his downtime, Aidan is an avid burrito enthusiast and has been frequenting the same burrito shop since he was old enough to chew. He lives in the San Francisco Bay Area with his two dogs, Lewis and June. (And yes, June does want her own book as well. They are discussing terms.)